tiger tales

5 River Road, Suite 128, Wilton, CT 06897
Published in the United States 2019
Originally published in Great Britain 2019
Text copyright © 2019 Little Tiger Press Ltd.
Illustrations copyright © 2017 Genine Delahaye
ISBN-13: 978-1-68010-543-8
ISBN-10: 1-68010-543-4
Printed in China
LTP/2700/2453/0918
10 9 8 7 6 5 4 3 2 1

For more insight and activities, visit us at www.tigertalesbooks.com

You're My baby

Baby Record Book

tiger tales

Exciting News!

How Mommy found out she was expecting you:

We were most excited about:

The first people we told were:

....

....

....

We thought you were going to be a:

boy

girl

The First Time We Saw You

Mommy had her first ultrasound on:

....

This is what you looked like:

PLACE YOUR ULTRASOUND PHOTO HERE

We first heard your heartbeat on:

_____

And this is how we felt when we first saw you:

_____

_____

_____

Mommy first felt you kicking on:

_____

Waiting for You to Arrive...

Here is a picture of our family before you arrived:

PLACE YOUR FAMILY PHOTO HERE

Your due date was:

....

This is Mommy when she was expecting you:

PLACE YOUR FAVORITE PREGNANCY
PHOTO HERE!

These are some of the names we thought about calling you:

Boys' names

Girls' names

The Day You Were Born!

We knew you were ready to be born when:

....

....

You were born on:

....

The time was:

....

The place was:

....

....

You took

....

hours to be born.

You weighed:

When you were measured, you were

long.

Your hair color was:

Your eyes were:

The name we gave you is:

The name means:

We chose this special name because:

Your First Moments

When we first held you, this is how we felt:

....

This is the very first photograph of you:

PLACE YOUR FIRST PHOTO OF BABY HERE

Look how wonderful you are!

Here you are with us!

PLACE YOUR FIRST FAMILY PHOTO HERE!

We already can't imagine the world without you!

Welcome to the Family!

YOU!

The other special people in
your life are:

. . . .

. . . .

. . . .

The person you look like
the most is:

. . . .

PLACE A SPECIAL FAMILY PHOTO HERE

Early Days

This is a picture of your home:

You were allowed
to come home on:

....

ADD A PHOTO OF YOUR HOME HERE

And here's your bedroom, which we made cozy and comfy for you:

PLACE A PHOTO OF BABY'S ROOM HERE

This was the address of your first home:

---- ---- ---- ----

---- ---- ---- ----

---- ---- ---- ----

---- ---- ---- ----

Celebrating You!

We received so many sweet messages and cards for you.

These are some of the people who sent you cards:

. . . .

These people came to visit:

Some of the first presents you received were:

Tiny Fingers and Tiny Toes

These are your first handprints:

And these are your first footprints:

Aren't they tiny!

Getting to Know You

In your first weeks, we couldn't wait to get to know you better.

You ate _____ times a day.

Our favorite outfits for you were:

_____

_____

_____

_____

_____

Our favorite memories of your first weeks are:

_____

_____

_____

_____

Your favorite time
for cuddling was:

_____

Your First Times

You first slept through the night when you were _____ old.

Here is a picture of your beautiful smile!

PLACE A SPECIAL PHOTO OF BABY

SMILING HERE

The first person you waved to was:

_____

You first clapped your hands when you were _____ old.

You first held your head up when you were _____ old.

You first sat up by yourself when you were _____ old.

On the Move!

You started crawling when you were

_____ old.

You stood up on your own when you

were _____ old.

You took your first steps when you

were _____ old.

Look, you are walking!

This was the date: ---------------------

PLACE YOUR FAVORITE PHOTO OF BABY

WALKING HERE

Watching You Grow!

Three Months Old

Date: _____

Weight: _____

Height: _____

Six Months Old

Date: _____

Weight: _____

Height: _____

Nine Months Old

Date: _____

Weight: _____

Height: _____

One Year Old

Date: ----------------

Weight: ----------------

Height: ----------------

You are growing up so fast!

These are the things that have changed most in your first year:

And this is when your first tooth appeared:

Your Favorite Foods

You first tried solid food

when you were _____ old.

Here is our favorite picture of you eating:

PLACE YOUR PHOTO HERE

You liked these foods the most:

_____

_____

_____

_____

And you didn't like these:

_____

_____

_____

_____

You first held a cup when you were _____ old.

Your Playtime

Here is a picture of your favorite toy:

PLACE YOUR PHOTO HERE

Your other favorite toys were:

························

························

························

Our favorite book
to read together was:

....

You liked playing these games:

And when you heard
these songs, your little feet
started dancing:

Out and About

Your first outing was on:

....

We went on a fun adventure to:

....

....

....

You first went on vacation to:

_____

_____

_____

Here is a picture of you on vacation!

ADD YOUR FAVORITE VACATION

PHOTO HERE

Your First Words

Your very first word was:

....

These were the names you had for special things:

.... meant ....

.... meant ....

.... meant ....

.... meant ....

.... meant ....

Your favorite
rhymes and songs were:

Your First Christmas

You spent your first Christmas at:

....

....

....

You wore this special outfit:

....

....

....

These were the people who shared
your first Christmas with you:

....

....

....

....

....

And these were some of your favorite presents:

....

....

....

....

Your First Birthday

We can't believe you've been in the world for an entire year!

Here you are on your first birthday:

PLACE YOUR SPECIAL
1ST BIRTHDAY PHOTO HERE

Look how much you have changed!

The special friends who came
to see you were:

This is what we did on your first birthday:

Some of your favorite presents were:

Our Lasting Thoughts

We love you because:

You are so precious to us, little one.

Some of our most cherished memories are:

Thank you for being in our lives!

These are our hopes and dreams for you:

— — — — — — — — — — — — — — — — — — — —

— — — — — — — — — — — — — — — — — — — —

— — — — — — — — — — — — — — — — — — — —

Special keepsakes from Baby's first year